To Arthur and Gustav

Copyright © 2007 by Christoph Niemann

Published in the United States by Schwartz & Wade
Books, an imprint of Random House Children's Books,
a division of Random House, Inc., New York.

SCHWARTZ & WADE BOOKS and colophon are trademarks of
Random House, Inc.

www.randomhouse.com/kids

Educators and librarians, for a variety of teaching tools,
visit us at www.randomhouse.com/teachers

Library of Congress Cataloging-in-Publication Data
Niemann, Christoph.
  The police cloud / Christoph Niemann. — 1st ed.
     p. cm.
Summary: A small cloud that has always dreamed of
becoming a police officer discovers that he might not be
suited to the job.
ISBN 978-0-375-83963-4 (hardcover) —
ISBN 978-0-375-93963-1 (lib. bdg.)
 [1. Clouds—Fiction. 2. Police—Fiction.
3. Self-perception—Fiction.] I. Title.

  PZ7.N56848Pol 2007
  [E]—dc22
  2006006415

The text of this book is set in Whitman.
The characters and layered environments were created
and composed in Adobe Illustrator.
Book design by Rachael Cole

PRINTED IN CHINA

10 9 8 7 6 5 4 3 2 1

First Edition

THE POLICE
CLOUD

CHRISTOPH NIEMANN

schwartz & wade books · new york

There once was a cloud who lived in a big city. Ever since he had been a small puff, he had dreamed of being a police officer.

One day the cloud asked his friend, the
police helicopter, "Can you help me get a job
in the police department? I want to wear a big
blue hat and help people."

"I'll see what I can do," said the helicopter.

Together they went down to the station to see the police chief. "I don't think we've ever had a cloud work as a police officer, but I am willing to give you a try," he said.

And so it happened that the cloud's dream finally came true.

The first day on the job,
the cloud saw a burglar.

"Stop in the name of the law!"
he shouted, and moved in to help
the other officers.

Yet somehow the thief got away.

The next day, the cloud was assigned
to direct traffic at a busy intersection.

That didn't go
well, either.

"Maybe chasing burglars and directing traffic isn't for me," the cloud told the chief. "Is there anything else a police cloud can do?"

"You could work in the city park," the chief suggested. "You could help people who are lost and make sure everyone is safe and happy."

"That sounds perfect," said the cloud.

But as soon as the cloud began his patrol,
nobody seemed very happy.

"I guess I'm just not cut out to be a police cloud," said the cloud. And no matter how hard he tried not to, he began to cry. Then he dropped his police hat and slowly drifted away.

As he drifted, the cloud became sadder and sadder.
Soon tears were pouring down his cheeks.

He cried so hard that he couldn't hear a
burning house shouting for help.
"Save me! Save me!" it called out.

Without even knowing it, the cloud
came to the rescue!
"You're my hero," said the house.

When the firefighters arrived, they were very impressed to see what the cloud had done all by himself.

The fire chief came to congratulate the cloud.
"Do you want to join the fire department?" he asked.
"We could really use a cloud like you!"

"That sounds perfect,"
said the cloud . . .

. . . and it was.